JoJo & Bow Bow

JINGLE BOWS AND MISTLETOE

SUPER SPECIAL

BY JoJo Siwa

nickelodeon

AMULET BOOKS NEW YORK

Library of Congress Cataloging-in-Publication Data

Names: Siwa, JoJo, 2003- author.
Title: Jingle bows and mistletoe / by JoJo Siwa.
Description: New York : Nickelodeon/Amulet Books, [2020] | Series: JoJo and BowBow | Audience: Ages 6 to 9. | Summary: "It's the holiday season, and that means it's time for some of JoJo Siwa's absolute favorite things! Best of all, Michelle Lee has invited JoJo and her friends to spend winter break in Colorado for Michelle's ice dancing performance. There's hot cocoa, presents tied up with colorful bows, and sparkly snow everywhere in sight. But when something unexpected threatens to derail their frosty fun, JoJo and all of her friends will have to come together for one big holiday surprise"-- Provided by publisher.
Identifiers: LCCN 2020029403 | ISBN 9781419748646 (hardcover)
Classification: LCC PZ7.1.S574 Jin 2020 | DDC [E]--dc23
LC record available at https://lccn.loc.gov/2020029403

ISBN 978-1-4197-4864-6

Printed and bound in the United States
10 9 8 7 6 5 4 3 2

ABRAMS The Art of Books
195 Broadway, New York, NY 10007
abramsbooks.com

CONTENTS

CHAPTER 1..1

CHAPTER 2..25

CHAPTER 3..52

CHAPTER 4..76

CHAPTER 5..93

CHAPTER 6..123

CHAPTER 7..144

CHAPTER ONE

"Left," JoJo called up to her big brother, who was positioning a dollop of whipped cream with a cherry on top above the front door of their family home. "No, right. A little more right! Left again, just a smidge. Steady, steady. Oh no!" The cherry wobbled a little, then a little more, then toppled right off the metal lever her brother had been using to position it, and tumbled onto the ground—along with the whipped cream—with a *splat*.

Well, the *splat* was really just in JoJo's imagination, because it wasn't *real* whipped cream—it was just a Christmas decoration! JoJo's very favorite thing in the entire world was the fun of decorating her house for Christmas, and every single year her family went all out. This year, the house was covered in rainbows and sparkles and candy, almost like a gingerbread house. The whipped cream and cherry on top were only pretend, but that didn't stop them from looking delicious. And they were ultra-glittery, just the way JoJo liked her real whipped cream—with sugar sprinkles.

But now JoJo's brother was lying on the grass with the whipped cream beside him.

"Are you okay?" JoJo asked, holding out her hand to pull him up. Her brother had tumbled backward when the whipped cream fell, but the decoration was so soft that it couldn't have hurt even BowBow, JoJo's teeny-tiny teacup Yorkie.

"I'm fine," he said, standing and brushing off his shorts. It was December, but it was Los Angeles December, which meant they could still wear shorts and T-shirts on sunny days. In fact, JoJo wasn't sure what she was going to pack for her trip to Tinseltown Resort and Rink the following day! The resort was in the mountains, and it was bound to require the kind of cold-weather clothes JoJo didn't own a lot of, given the California heat.

BowBow yipped a few times at the whipped cream, then ran around at their feet. Finally she approached it cautiously and took a sniff, then a lick with her tiny tongue. BowBow growled, hopping backward.

JoJo laughed. "That's what you get for trying to sneak people food, BowBow!" she said. "Doggie treats for you later!"

"JoJo," said her brother, "Mom and Dad might have to help us with the whipped cream! Let's finish putting the lollipops along the walkway in the meantime."

"Sure thing, Hansel," JoJo answered.

"Okay, Gretel."

The rest of the house was totally something out of a fairy tale—it was a candy-coated winter wonderland that JoJo called 'Sweet Land!' There was a lollipop-covered garage, gingerbread on the side of the house and gingerbread men lining the front walkway, and dozens of light-up trees. And that was just the beginning. The inside of the house was just as fancy! JoJo's closest friends—Kyra, Grace, Miley, and Jacob—were coming over for a Secret Santa gift swap

later on, and she wanted everything to be perfect for their arrival.

Just as they put the finishing touches on the lollipop-lined walkway, Miley's mom pulled up.

"Yoo-hoo!" she shouted, rolling down her window. "I know it's nearly seventy degrees out today, but I feel like I'm in the North Pole when I'm at your house. Talk about Christmas spirit!"

"Hi, Mrs. McKenna!" JoJo smiled at her BFF's mom, who was basically her second mom. "Hi, Miley! Hi, Grace, Kyra, and Jacob!"

"Hi, kids," Mrs. McKenna said to JoJo and her brother, giving them a wave. Then she said goodbye to Miley and the others as they slid out of the car. "Be good, everyone! Enjoy your Frosty Flip." She winked and smiled. "Miley, I'll be back to pick you and JoJo up at ten o'clock tomorrow morning and take you to the airport. Jacob, your dad said he'd give the rest of you kids a lift home in a few hours." JoJo was excited for a sleepover with her BFF—she and Miley had a lot to discuss! Their mountain adventure the next day had been arranged by their friend Michelle Lee, the famous ice dancer. Michelle had invited the whole group, but Grace was visiting her grandmother for the week, Jacob was going to the Bahamas with his parents and baby brother, and Kyra was hosting her cousins at home. They were all sad to miss the Tinseltown trip, but everyone's plans for the holiday were so exciting that no one could really complain!

"Mom." Miley rolled her eyes. "It's Secret Santa, not a Frosty Flip!" JoJo giggled and waved as Mrs. McKenna pulled out of the driveway and headed back down the block toward Miley's house, which was just around the corner. Mrs. McKenna was always making silly jokes. Miley pretended to be annoyed, but JoJo knew she not-so-secretly thought her mom was the coolest and funniest.

"Have fun, you guys," JoJo's brother told them. "I've got to get ready for baseball practice."

JoJo's friends said goodbye to him, then scattered around the yard to examine the decorations.

"Oh, JoJo, this is even better than last year!" exclaimed Grace.

"I know! We really went all out," JoJo told her. "People driving by have been stopping to see! You know how much I love Christmas. Wait'll you see the inside of the house. But Jacob, your hands are full. Let me help you," she said, reaching for a foil-wrapped tray that Jacob held in one hand. He carried a wrapped gift for their Secret Santa exchange in the other.

"I think you'll like what's inside that tray!" Miley piped in.

"I don't know if I'm more curious about the present or the contents of this tray," JoJo teased. "Am I right that there's something yummy inside?"

"Only his latest and greatest concoction!" Kyra said. Jacob was a budding pastry chef— he'd even been in national competitions and on TV!

"I sampled one on the way." Grace looked a little guilty, her pale skin flushing pink, making her freckles stand out.

"All I can say is, *yummm*," Miley said with a wink.

"I can't stand the suspense!" JoJo exclaimed. She peeked under the tinfoil to see what was inside. Then she gasped in delight.

"Jacob, you didn't!"

The tray was chock-full of an assortment of all JoJo's very favorite Christmas cookies. JoJo led her friends inside and placed the tray on the kitchen table, while they *ooh*-ed and *ahh*-ed over the decorations, which included several themed Christmas trees standing six feet tall each.

"Is that . . . a movie theater tree?!" Miley asked wonderingly.

"Sure is!" JoJo told her, laughing. "And all those candy decorations are real! We've got Milk Duds and Sour Patch Kids and everything!"

"There's even a movie reel ornament!" Grace squealed and clapped her hands.

"Okay, is it just me or is this Grinch tree ah-mazing?" Kyra wanted to know. She pointed at an upside-down tree with red and green decorations, a sign that read

"Who-ville," and a Grinch on top. "JoJo, this is so cool! Did you come up with these ideas yourself?"

"My whole family did!" JoJo explained. "You know we *love* crafts and other creative things. We even have a craft room. But the movie theater tree was all me, of course. Because, movie candy, obviously! And check out the popcorn on top."

"Personally I'm into the flamingo tree," Jacob said, pointing to an enormous pink tree with a flamingo on top. "And I'm obsessed with all the bows everywhere. Good work, JoJo."

"Represent." JoJo agreed. "I'm so glad you guys are into it! The rainbow trees are my personal faves. It's basically a JoJo forest in here," she said with a laugh. "I'm just glad my family is as into it as I am! But let's have some cookies and start the

Secret Santa. Or, wait, what did your mom call it, Miley?"

"'Frosty Flip,'" Miley told her with a grin. "She's such a nerd."

"But a lovable nerd," JoJo broke in. "I like that—'Frosty Flip.' I'm so glad you guys were willing to do our exchange early this year, instead of right before Christmas like usual."

"Well, with all our family schedules we didn't have much choice," Grace pointed out. "But there's nothing better than stretching out Christmas as long as possible, right?"

"Right!" Kyra agreed. "It wouldn't be the same without our friend tradition."

"Let's all put our gifts under the flamingo tree," JoJo suggested. "We can open them after dinner." Everyone pulled out their gifts—all wrapped in red tissue paper, so no one would know who their Secret Santa was—and placed them under the pink flamingo tree. Then they followed JoJo into the kitchen.

JoJo was unwrapping Jacob's cookies when her mom came in.

"Cookies before dinner!" she exclaimed. "I approve . . . at least during Christmas week. I ordered you pizza too—it should be here in an hour."

JoJo gave her mom a hug. "You know us so well," she told her.

"I sure do," Mrs. Siwa agreed. "I'm off to work on some bows for your next show, JoJo—I'll be in the craft room if you need me! And your dad is in the basement watching TV."

"Sounds good, but I think we've got this covered," JoJo said. "Thanks, Mom! You're the best." JoJo turned back to Jacob's sweet treats. There were dozens of sugar cut-out cookies in the shape of candy canes,

Christmas trees, and snowmen. And there were tiny sandwich cookies sprinkled with sugar and filled with pink cream. There were cranberry bars, and seven-layer bars thick with coconut, graham cracker, and chocolate chips. JoJo loved all of Jacob's baking, but his Christmas cookies were best of all.

"There's frosting and sprinkles for decorating the cutout cookies," Jacob explained. "Maybe we can do that before the pizza arrives!"

"That sounds perfect," Grace exclaimed. "I love decorating cookies!"

JoJo put wax paper down on the kitchen table, and the five friends dug into tubs of frosting Jacob pulled from his backpack. Jacob had brought red, green, and white frosting as well as edible glitter in silver and gold, and sprinkles in all colors.

JoJo was putting the finishing touches on a snowman when she looked over at Kyra. Her friend had a big glob of green frosting on one finger, and her own cookie was untouched.

"Kyra," JoJo laughed. "You're doing more frosting-eating than decorating!"

Kyra looked guilty, but then giggled. "I can't help it! My sweet tooth is addicted to this amazing frosting! Jacob, you did it again—everything you make is the absolute best."

Half an hour later, all the cookies were frosted. Grace had even made a striped scarf for her snowman, using frosting and sprinkles.

"Grace, I knew you were an amazing artist, but those cookies look professional," exclaimed Kyra.

"Well, your snowmen are little fashionistas," Grace shot back. JoJo laughed. It was true—Kyra was a budding fashion designer, and all of her snowmen were wearing tiny, glittery overalls! Every single one of her friends was super talented.

Just then, the doorbell rang—it was the pizza!

"Perfect timing," JoJo exclaimed. "Mom, pizza's here!"

Mrs. Siwa emerged from the craft room and answered the door, then brought back two steaming large pizzas. She opened them up on the kitchen table, and the kids dug in.

"Wait for plates!" Mrs. Siwa called, but there was no stopping JoJo and her friends when they were hungry! By the time Mrs. Siwa brought plates over, JoJo was already half finished with her first slice of delicious pepperoni pizza. "Sorry, Mom!" she said. BowBow barked twice from beside her.

"BowBow, you have Pupperoni!" JoJo exclaimed. She took another bite of the pizza, then went to the pantry where Bow-Bow's treats were kept. "Don't worry, we'd never leave you out!"

"Let me!" Miley exclaimed, wiping off her mouth. JoJo handed Miley the treat, and Miley asked BowBow to sit pretty, then shake, then roll over. BowBow did all her tricks like a good girl, and Miley gave the dog a treat.

After pizza, it was time for eating their cookie masterpieces and the grand finale of the night: Secret Santa! The kids rushed to the flamingo tree. Secret Santa was a tradition they looked forward to for the entire year. At Friendsgiving—the Thanksgiving party Miley threw the day after Thanksgiving—they drew names. Then they had a whole month to dream up the perfect gift for that person. This year, JoJo had drawn Grace's name. She couldn't wait for Grace to open it!

"Let's open in alphabetical order," Grace suggested thoughtfully.

"That means you're first, Grace!" Kyra exclaimed. "That long tube-shaped one has your name on it."

Grace eagerly unwrapped the gift, while JoJo watched. JoJo liked giving gifts even better than getting them, and this was no exception. Finally Grace pulled all the paper off, leaving only a long, cardboard tube. She popped the lid off the tube and pulled out the contents. JoJo held her breath as Grace unfurled her gift. When she'd spread it out flat, she gasped.

"It's a caticorn poster!" she exclaimed. "I love it."

"Not just a caticorn poster," JoJo piped in. "But a caticorn poster illustrated by your artist idol—and look, it's signed!"

Grace spotted the signature in the righthand corner. "Oh my gosh, oh my gosh, oh my gosh," she murmured. "JoJo, did you do this? This is the *best*, most thoughtful gift I've ever received! Or at least top five!"

"I'll take it," JoJo said, laughing. "Okay Jacob, you're up."

Jacob got a hilarious apron with all his friends' faces screen printed on it. "To carry us with you always," said Miley with a wink.

JoJo got a friendship album from Kyra, filled with Polaroid photos of their friendship and lots of adorable stickers decorating it. "I totally forgot about the time you filled my shoe with slime," JoJo said, looking at one of the photos through fits of giggles. "Best prank ever!"

"Best *friends* ever," Kyra corrected.

Kyra got two bolts of beautiful printed fabrics from Jacob. "I'll make a dress," she squealed.

And Miley got new glitter earbuds from Grace.

"You guys, each one of these gifts is perfect," Miley remarked. "We know each other so well."

"I agree," JoJo said, looking at her friends' smiling faces. "We're the luckiest."

An hour after the rest of their friends cleared out, Miley and JoJo put on their pjs, brushed their teeth, and headed into JoJo's room for bed. JoJo pulled her carry-on suitcase from her closet and began packing for her big adventure with Miley. They were leaving the next day, and she didn't have a moment to lose. Their trip was going to be nothing short of a winter wonderland. And the best part of all was that BowBow was joining them! The ski resort where the friends were headed was dog friendly, and BowBow was tiny enough to ride on the plane in a carry-on doggie bag.

"I don't have enough cold-weather stuff," she mentioned to Miley, pulling out two sweatshirts and a pair of jeans. "What are we going to wear on the slopes?"

"Mrs. Lee said she'd bring extra of Michelle's things," Miley reminded JoJo. "I can't wait to take skiing lessons at the resort! I've never even seen snow!"

"You're such a California girl," JoJo teased. "But I know what you mean. Growing up with snow was so magical, especially around the holidays. I love that we're going to have a white Christmas!" JoJo spent her childhood in Omaha before she moved to Los Angeles,

21

so she'd been used to snow—and loving it—since she was a little kid making snow angels.

"Well, we'll be back in LA for Christmas," Miley reminded JoJo, helping her stuff some socks into the suitcase.

"Yes, but you know what I mean. It'll get us in the Christmas spirit."

"I'm excited to see Michelle perform as lead ice dancer in *The Snow Queen on Ice*," Miley said, changing the subject. "She told me there will be a public skate right after dress rehearsal, and that we can rent skates there. You know how I love to skate!"

"I sure do! Just don't get hurt this time," JoJo said, reminding Miley of the time she hurt her ankle on the ice just before her birthday. They'd had to cancel her ice-skating party, but JoJo and the others had thrown her a surprise slumber party instead, and it had been tons of fun.

"I promise," Miley said, grinning. "Besides, I'm much better than before! I've been taking lessons."

"Miley! I have an idea," JoJo told her. "Let's pack holiday costumes to wear when we go ice-skating! How fun would that be?"

"Super fun!" Miley exclaimed. "But I don't think I have anything. Can I borrow something of yours?"

"Duh," JoJo told Miley. "I have a super cute costume from one of my holiday shows last year that you can borrow, and I have a costume I was planning to wear on tour this year that I can use. We'll bring the holiday cheer!"

"I can't wait," Miley said. "But JoJo, are you almost done packing?" She yawned, and climbed up on JoJo's bed. "My mom is going to be here bright and early to take us to the airport!"

"Yep, almost ready! Just one last thing . . ." JoJo walked over to her closet and selected a dozen bows from her ginormous bow collection. Then, as an afterthought, she grabbed an outfit from BowBow's wardrobe and tossed it in with the rest.

"Only the sparkliest bows for Tinseltown Resort and Rink!" She winked at Miley, but Miley was already asleep, sprawled across the bed, her mouth hanging half open. Just then, Miley let out a big snore.

JoJo stifled a giggle, then closed her suitcase and zipped it up. There was no one she'd rather go on an adventure with than Miley, snores and all.

CHAPTER TWO

"**P**lease buckle your seat belts and put your tray tables in a locked and upright position," said the flight attendant. JoJo checked her belt—it was secure. Miley fiddled with the clip on her tray table, and JoJo reached over to help her. BowBow was nestled in her carrier at JoJo's feet, being a good girl.

"Thanks, JoJo," Miley said. "This is only my third time flying, can you believe it? Do you think we'll get snacks?"

"Probably pretzels or cookies," Michelle weighed in from across the aisle. "But not until we're in the air."

Two hours earlier, Miley's mom had dropped Miley and JoJo at the airport, where they'd met Mrs. Lee and Michelle. JoJo *loved* airports, but they hadn't had much time to look around—they were in a rush! Miley had kissed her mom goodbye and then Mrs. Lee had whisked all three girls through security. At security, JoJo's glitter high-tops had been tagged for a closer inspection.

"I've never seen shoes this sparkly," commented the security agent as she conducted her thorough check. "Lots of bling, but clean as a whistle!" Then she'd handed the shoes back to JoJo, and they were off.

Now they were buckled up and ready to go! JoJo leaned over to slip BowBow a treat. BowBow loved flying almost as much as she did.

"Weather is beautiful in LA, as usual," the pilot said over the loudspeaker as the plane began to taxi—a fancy word for moving down the runway to get in line for flight. "But a storm's a-brewing up north! Conditions for takeoff and landing are healthy, folks. We're going to be just ahead of any snowfall. We're next in line for takeoff. Buckle up and enjoy the flight."

"A storm?" Miley looked worried. Mrs. Lee smiled at her reassuringly from across the aisle, where she sat with Michelle.

"Don't worry, sweetie," she said. "The pilot told us we're safe, and fresh snow means fresh powder for the slopes, which makes for better skiing. This is really good news."

"Okay." Miley smiled. "I've just never seen snow, let alone a snowstorm! I'm not sure what to expect."

"You're going to love it," JoJo told her. She was so excited to share the fun of snow with Miley!

"Totally!" said Michelle. "And you already like ice-skating, so you're almost certain to like other snow activities. Like skiing."

"And snowball fights," put in JoJo.

"And snow forts," added Mrs. Lee. "The resort has a huge outdoor space—there will be loads to do in the snow!"

"Doesn't it get cold?" Miley wanted to know, looking worried.

"Sure, but that's why we bundle up," Michelle explained. "And in the mountains it's really sunny—so even though the air is cold, you won't be uncomfortable during the day. Sometimes I even take my jacket off to walk around town! Sometimes I even get ice cream! There's a cute downtown area with shops and stuff."

"How many times have you ice-danced at Tinseltown, Michelle?" JoJo really admired Michelle, who was world famous for her ice-dancing, but just about as down-to-earth as they came.

"This'll be my third time," Michelle told them. "But I've only ever done *The Nutcracker*. *The Snow Queen on Ice* is new this year, and I'm really looking forward to changing it up."

Just then, the plane started moving faster. They were about to take off! JoJo looked at Miley, who had turned a little pale. She clasped her friend's hand in hers.

"Don't worry," JoJo said to Miley. "Flying is perfectly safe. It's this first part—taking off—that's the scariest!"

Sure enough, soon they were in the air, and Miley—who had chosen the window seat—was craning her neck to see all the buildings and trees shrinking smaller and smaller the higher they went. "So cool," she breathed. "Look, JoJo! You can see Griffith Observatory!" JoJo craned her neck, but they were too high. They were already soaring through wisps of clouds.

"I can't believe we are already this high in the air." Miley looked impressed. From beneath JoJo's feet, BowBow yipped in agreement.

"BowBow was *born* to fly," JoJo laughed.

Then the captain came back on. "We are about to turn off the FASTEN SEAT BELT sign, so you can move around the cabin," he explained. "And soon we'll start the beverage and snack service. It's clear skies up here and we'll be landing in a quick two hours."

Michelle was snacking on popcorn and reading a magazine, and her mom had already dozed off against the window on their side of the plane. JoJo didn't want to snooze—she wanted to soak it all in!

"Want to watch a movie?" she asked Miley.

"I would," Miley said, "but I forgot my earbuds in my suitcase."

"We can share mine! You take right and I get left. I did this with my mom once. Trust me, it'll be fun."

The two girls scrolled through their entertainment options on the backs of the seats in front of them. It was pretty cool having your own personal mini–movie theater! Finally they settled on a movie neither of them had seen yet.

"It's kind of an old one, but Grace told me it was good," JoJo mentioned, as she popped in the left earbud.

"Well Grace has amazing taste in movies," Miley acknowledged, "thanks to her big sister's recommendations. So I bet we're in for a treat." Grace's big sister was an artist who was already in college, and she knew all the coolest stuff. JoJo and her friends were always finding the best music, movies, clothes, and shows through Penny.

"Okay, on the count of three, we both press Play at the same time," JoJo told Miley. Both girls' index fingers hovered over the Play buttons on the screens in front of them.

"One . . . ," JoJo said.

"Two . . . ," Miley continued.

"Three!" they said together, punching Play. They looked at each other and smiled. JoJo and Miley were almost always in perfect accord.

"We probably could have done that with our eyes closed and earbuds in," JoJo told her friend. But Miley was already immersed in the film.

Partway through the movie, during a dramatic hot air balloon scene, the flight attendants came through with snacks.

"We have a special holiday surprise!" they told the girls and Mrs. Lee. "Free candy!"

"Hurray!" cheered JoJo. "This is a plane after my own heart!" She picked out some of her favorite chocolates along with a soda and relaxed back in for the remainder of the flight.

A short while later, they touched down at their destination.

"Phew!" Miley said, as the plane rolled to a stop. "I wasn't even scared at all during landing."

JoJo laughed. "It would be okay if you were a little scared," she assured her friend. In fact, Miley had been clutching JoJo's hand again the whole way down. JoJo looked over at Michelle, who was rubbing sleep from her eyes while Mrs. Lee gathered up their magazines and snack wrappers.

"We both got a good nap in, didn't we, sweetie?" Mrs. Lee said to Michelle. "That's good. You'll need your rest for *The Snow Queen on Ice*. Dress rehearsal is at 8 A.M. sharp tomorrow!"

"Is that when we have our ski lessons?" JoJo asked Mrs. Lee. Around them, the other passengers were unbuckling their seat belts and reaching for their belongings.

"Nope, you two can sleep in. I scheduled you a beginners' lesson at ten."

"Awesome!" JoJo exclaimed. Then she blushed. JoJo was always so busy that she loved to sleep in when she could!

The group stepped off the plane, gathered their carry-on bags in the planeside corridor, and made their way through the airport and outside, where there was already a car waiting to pick them up.

"Are you Mrs. Lee and Michelle?" the driver asked.

"Yes, and these are our friends Miley and JoJo," Mrs. Lee replied. The driver took everyone's bags and held open the door to the SUV.

"Hop in," she said. "It's just about twenty minutes to the resort."

While they were making the winding trip into the mountains, they played some of JoJo's greatest hits on her iPhone. They belted out the words to "Boomerang," then "Hold the Drama," then "Every Girl's a Super Girl" and were just about to start into "D.R.E.A.M." when they turned on to a long, winding drive and into a quaint village lined with hotels that looked more like gingerbread houses. Miley's nose was glued to the window the whole way, and even though JoJo had seen a ton of snow in her lifetime, she was impressed too. It was as if someone had dumped vanilla frosting with sparkly white sugar sprinkles all over Tinseltown.

"Here we are!" cheered Michelle. "My favorite place on earth! Look, that's where we'll be staying!" She pointed toward a beautiful brick building that looked like a snow-topped palace.

The producers of *The Snow Queen on Ice* had pulled out all the stops for Michelle, her mom, and their guests' lodging. Michelle had told JoJo and Miley how cool it was, but JoJo was amazed.

"Wow," Miley breathed. "This is gorgeous!" BowBow gave a bark of agreement.

"You know who else has never seen snow before?" JoJo asked. "This girl!" She pointed at BowBow, who poked her nose against the mesh of her carrier. BowBow snuffled and yipped excitedly.

"I bet she's going to love it," Mrs. Lee interjected. "Our dog, Shiny—short for Sunshine, Michelle named her—used to be crazy for snow when we lived in Indiana."

"Shiny was obsessed with snow! She was like a little rabbit hopping in and out of it," Michelle added. "She would get so excited every winter."

"What happened to Shiny? Why haven't we met her?" JoJo asked. They'd been to Michelle's house a few times and had met a dog called Hal (short for Halibut) and a cat named Rory, but never a Shiny.

"Oh, she went to doggie heaven when I was twelve," Michelle said, looking sad.

"She was Mr. Lee's and my dog before Michelle and her sister were born," explained

Mrs. Lee. "She lived to a ripe old age and brought us tons of love."

JoJo smiled—it seemed like Shiny had been cherished by the Lee family. Then she took a moment to unzip BowBow's carrier and scratch her ears. She was glad BowBow was still a young dog, with a long life ahead of her.

The driver pulled into a parking spot and cut the engine. "Welcome to Tinseltown Resort and Rink, girls!" Mrs. Lee said. "Let the fun begin!"

"**O**kay, we are *definitely* going straight back down to that lobby the second we're done unpacking," JoJo informed the others, as she placed folded shirts and jeans into a long wooden bureau.

"I'm in! Did you see that hot cocoa bar?" Miley wanted to know.

"It's the best," Michelle agreed. "They even have homemade, jumbo-size marshmallows. I could live on hot cocoa for our entire trip." The girls giggled.

"But let's take a sec to enjoy this hotel situation first," JoJo pointed out. *The Snow Queen on Ice* had set them up with an entire suite consisting of two interconnected bedrooms, two bathrooms, and a lounge area complete with a foosball table! Best of all— at least according to JoJo and BowBow: There was a cozy doggie bed in one corner of their room, two doggie dishes, and a bag of dog treats on top of the bureau, tied with a red ribbon.

"BowBow, you're getting the royal treatment!" she told her pup. Then, to Michelle and Miley, she said, "Have you guys ever been on a bed so fancy?" JoJo took a running start and leapt onto one of two enormous beds, each of which could comfortably fit them all. The beds had wooden frames with tall poles in every corner and canopies draped on top.

"Or a bed so *bouncy?*" asked Miley, leaping on next to her. Then Michelle came running over and took a flying leap onto the space next to them, causing Miley and JoJo to bounce in the air as if they were on a trampoline. BowBow ran circles on the carpeted floor below, barking happily.

Then Miley got a sparkle in her eye.

"Uh-oh," JoJo said. She knew Miley, and that sparkle meant trouble! But it was too late. Her choreographer BFF was on her feet and bouncing around the bed, showcasing some of her favorite dance moves. Michelle looked at JoJo and shrugged as if to say *Why not?* Then all three girls were jumping on the

bed and dancing around, letting loose fits of giggles.

"What is going on here?"

Mrs. Lee poked her head in from the doorway to the adjoining room, where she would be sleeping.

"Girls!" She put her hands on her hips. "You can't jump on the bed! It isn't safe, and you might break something."

JoJo plopped back down, embarrassed. Mrs. Lee was right. And JoJo always tried to be a good guest.

"Sorry, Mrs. Lee," she said. "It won't happen again."

Miley and Michelle plopped next to her, breathless. "Sorry," they echoed.

Mrs. Lee relaxed her arms and smiled. "Well, I *am* glad you're having so much fun," she told them. "It's nearly dinner time. What do you say we head downstairs and grab some food, then hit up the hot chocolate bar? You can bring it back to the room while you relax before bed."

"Sounds great!"

The girls followed Mrs. Lee downstairs to a restaurant that was lined all in glass. Colorful red-and-green garlands hung everywhere, there was a tree with brightly colored lights in one corner, and carols played through overhead speakers.

"What's that?" Miley asked JoJo, pointing at a shrub hanging from a ribbon at the restaurant's entrance. It was green with what appeared to be white berries.

"Mistletoe!" JoJo recognized it from her own home. "It's for kissing!"

"Ewww." Miley made a grossed-out face. "You kiss it?"

"No, no." JoJo laughed. "It's a symbol of love. If you walk under it at the same time as someone you love, you're supposed to kiss them! My parents are always 'accidentally' walking under it at home," she said, using air quotes.

"I still think it's gross," Miley insisted, turning her attention to the floor-to-ceiling windows that covered one whole side of the restaurant and overlooked the skating rink, with the mountains behind it. "So cool," she breathed. The ice rink was open to the public, and just then, lots of families were skating to the tunes of a DJ set up in a booth nearby. Some skiers were still on the slopes, weaving around and in front of one another in wavy patterns.

"Wow. This is a really amazing view," JoJo agreed.

"Why don't they ski straight down?" Miley wanted to know.

Mrs. Lee laughed, tuning into the conversation. "You'll learn tomorrow," she assured Miley. "But if you skied straight down, you would gain speed, and eventually you would be going too fast. Weaving from side-to-side like that slows you down and helps you control your descent."

"That sounds hard," Miley said. "I'm always up for a challenge, but maybe I'd also be okay hanging out right here!"

"Give it a try," Mrs. Lee suggested. "And if you don't like it, there's lots to do indoors. In fact, there's a whole program of holiday activities! I'll show you three the schedule when we get back upstairs."

JoJo was excited to ski, and they were only in the resort until the morning of Christmas Eve—that gave them two full days. She wanted to skate too, and they'd be watching

Michelle's performance the day after next, and of course she wanted to play in the snow with Miley and BowBow. This vacation was going to be jam-packed with fun!

"Can I help you?" asked the hostess, interrupting JoJo's thoughts.

"We'd like a table for four, please," Mrs. Lee asked. "Is there anything by the windows?"

"Coming right up," assured the hostess. "Follow me!"

Once they were seated, the waitress came over and handed them their menus. When JoJo accepted hers with a smile, the waitress paused.

"Wait a sec. JoJo Siwa, right?" she asked. "Yep, I'd know you anywhere! My daughter is such a huge fan."

"Cool!" said JoJo. "Would you like a selfie to send her?"

The waitress brightened. "I would love that! My name is Francie, by the way," she said to the group.

"These are my friends Michelle, Miley, and Mrs. Lee," JoJo explained. "What's your daughter's name?"

"Abigail," said Francie. "I'm so sorry to interrupt your meal—are you sure you don't mind posing for a quick selfie?"

"Not at all," JoJo said sincerely. "I live for this!" It was true. JoJo loved meeting her fans, and loved making kids happy. She would never turn down a chance to make someone's day.

"Will Abigail be around the resort at all this week?" Mrs. Lee asked, after JoJo and Francie had taken a quick snap. "Because we have guest passes to *The Snow Queen on Ice* in two days."

"Really?" Francie's eyes widened. "That's so kind of you! Abigail would love to go."

"Michelle is one of the leads!" exclaimed Miley.

"Wow, you must be an excellent skater," Francie said. "The best ice dancers in the world perform in that show! Francie would love to see it—she wants to be an ice dancer when she gets a little older."

"It's never too early to start," Michelle told Francie. "And in fact, some of the cast are giving free lessons to kids after our dress rehearsal tomorrow. Abigail should come!"

As Michelle and Francie exchanged information, JoJo took a peek at the menu. Her stomach was suddenly rumbling from the long day of travel.

"I'll let you take another minute to look at the menu before I take your order," said Francie, when she and Michelle were finished.

"No!" shouted Miley, Michelle, and JoJo in unison. Then they collapsed into giggles.

"What we mean is, we're ready to order now, if that's okay," JoJo explained.

"I've got some hungry kids on my hands," Mrs. Lee told Francie. "JoJo, why don't you start?"

JoJo and Miley both ordered mac and cheese, and Michelle ordered eggplant parm. "I'll have the salmon," said Mrs. Lee, rounding out their orders.

"Got it!" Francie headed off toward the kitchen, and JoJo stared out the window at the skiers, who all looked so confident on the slopes. JoJo was a good athlete in her own right and had been dancing since she was in diapers. To her, skiing looked like a graceful dance, and she couldn't wait to try it!

When their food came, the girls ate quickly, and at the end of the meal, Francie came out with a surprise.

"Happy holidays!" she said. "And thank you all for being so sweet about my little Abigail. Now—does everyone like chocolate?" She placed a giant slice of chocolate cake with ice cream in the middle of the table, and everyone cheered. "On the house!"

By the time they'd polished off what was definitely the world's best cake, all three girls were happy and tired.

"I never thought I'd say this, but I think we need to save the hot cocoa bar for tomorrow," Michelle told her mom. "I am stuffed!"

"Me too," JoJo exclaimed. "That cake was delish."

"Me three," said Miley. "How is it only seven o'clock? I'm going into a food coma!"

"There's plenty of time for hot cocoa and everything else you three want to do," Mrs. Lee told them. "How about we go upstairs and play a little foosball and get ready for bed? Tomorrow is a big day."

"And after that is another big day, and then *Christmas Eve!*" shouted JoJo. She was already having an amazing time with her friends, and she couldn't wait to go home and celebrate Christmas with her family. *This is the best week ever*, thought JoJo, as she filled BowBow's dishes with water and kibble, then took her place at the foosball machine. *What could go wrong?*

CHAPTER THREE

The next morning when JoJo woke up, BowBow's head was right next to hers on her pillow, while Miley snored beside her. Michelle's bed was rumpled but empty—she must have already left for dress rehearsal, thought JoJo. JoJo picked up her phone. It said nine o'clock, but she'd have had no idea otherwise—the curtains were drawn and the room was dark.

"BowBow," JoJo whispered to her fluffy pup. "Your bed is on the floor! How did you get all the way up here? Do you have wings I don't know about?" BowBow looked at JoJo innocently, then licked her cheek with her little pink tongue. JoJo laughed. "Okay, Bow-Bow, you're forgiven. But it's time to rise and shine." BowBow stretched her little legs over her head, lifting her tummy in the air for JoJo to scratch.

JoJo swung her legs over the bed and went to the bathroom to brush her teeth. When she got back, Miley was yawning and beginning to sit up.

"It feels like night in here," Miley remarked, climbing out of bed and moving to the window. "Let's open the curtains."

JoJo grabbed one curtain and Miley grabbed the other, and they pulled in opposite directions until the windows were exposed and light filtered into the room. JoJo gasped. She could hardly see outside, even with the curtains open. It was a whiteout!

"Oh *no*," Miley exclaimed. "Is this what a blizzard looks like?"

"I'm not sure," JoJo replied. "But it's definitely more snow than I've ever seen before!"

JoJo heard a knock on the door that separated their room from Mrs. Lee's.

"Girls, are you decent?" Mrs. Lee called.

"Come on in," Miley and JoJo shouted.

Mrs. Lee slipped into the room looking like she'd been awake for several hours already. She was wearing a flannel button-down, jeans, and sneakers, and her hair was pulled back into a chic ponytail.

"The snowstorm has started," she said, "just like our pilot yesterday said. But the forecast says it'll let up in plenty of time for our flight back to LA two days from now, so don't worry about that. I called your ski instructor and they said your lesson is still on for ten o'clock, so you have a little bit of time to eat breakfast and get dressed."

"Okay," JoJo said. "Is Michelle practicing in this weather?"

"The dress rehearsal was moved to an indoor rink," explained Mrs. Lee. "And if the weather doesn't let up by tomorrow, that's where the show will be as well. Now why don't I order you two some room service pancakes while you get ready? I can take BowBow out for her morning walk, so you're sure to be on time."

"Thanks, Mrs. Lee," JoJo said.

"Pancakes sound great," agreed Miley.

A few minutes later, they were bundled in turtlenecks and long johns layered under snow pants borrowed from Michelle. Mrs. Lee came back with a snow-covered Bow-Bow just as their breakfast was arriving.

"Yum, pancakes!" Miley exclaimed, as the cart of food was delivered to their room. She lifted the silver lid covering the platter and buried her nose in the steam. "Is that chocolate chip I smell?"

"Your favorite," said Mrs. Lee. "I remember from when we all went to the beach together!" Mrs. Lee was toweling BowBow off in the girls' bathroom.

"That is so sweet," JoJo said. "They're my favorite too. But here, let me take BowBow duty." She took the wriggly, wet pup from Mrs. Lee. "How did she do outside?"

"She loved the snow!" Mrs. Lee exclaimed. "A true snow bunny. You girls will have to take her out when you're done with your lesson—you'll get a kick out of her. Speaking of bunnies, we should head over to the bunny slope in about fifteen minutes. That's the beginner slope where your lesson will be held."

Twenty minutes later, both girls were standing in full puffy-coated snow gear at the top of the slope. JoJo was excited but nervous. The gently sloping "bunny hill" looked a lot steeper from way up top! Mrs. Lee had helped them clip their rental boots into their rental skis, and had ridden the chairlift with them and made sure they were okay getting off. But JoJo had nearly stumbled—it was scary getting off a moving bench, especially since the chair just sort of . . . kept going! There wasn't a lot of time to catch your balance. But JoJo's motto had always been to brush herself off and try again, no matter how many times she stumbled.

"You're going to want to glide forward with your weight on the inner edge of your skis," the instructor was saying, bending his knees inward to show them. "Keep your feet shoulder-width apart with your knees slightly bent." The snow was coming down in great big whorls, and JoJo was having trouble seeing the bottom of the hill. Miley gave her a panicked look, her eyes wide behind her ski mask.

Then the instructor—whose name was Rob—taught them how to keep their balance and how to form a wedge with their skis in order to control their speed. Next, he said he would hold each of their hands and lead them through a slow wedge partway down the slope. "Call it a pizza slice or a snowplow!" he said. JoJo went first, and during her turn, she giggled the whole way down, keeping her feet angled in the pizza wedge shape and loving the way her skis cut through the fresh snow.

"Wait here," Rob told her. Then he unclipped his skis and walked back up the slope to help Miley down. JoJo had to squint to see through the snow, but what she *did* see made her nervous. Miley fell twice, and the second time, she seemed to want to stay sitting. JoJo couldn't completely tell what was happening, but it looked like she was having trouble getting to her feet. Finally Rob and Miley caught up with JoJo.

"Are you okay?" JoJo asked her friend.

"No," Miley said. "JoJo, I'm glad I tried, but I *really* don't like skiing."

"That's okay," JoJo reassured her. "We're almost to the bottom. Do you think you can make it the rest of the way?"

"I can try," Miley said. "But I'm scared."

"I'll be with you the whole way," Rob told her. "If you fall, I'll catch you!"

"I'll be with you too," JoJo said. "Rob, I think I can try the wedge on my own now."

"Okay," he said, nodding. "This is the softest snow you'll ever see, so if you fall, you'll be fine."

"I might just need help getting back up," JoJo said with a giggle.

"No problem," Rob said. "Let's do this!"

But Miley stood there, not budging.

"I don't know if I can," she finally whispered. JoJo could see that her eyes were brimming slightly behind her mask. She put a gloved hand on her friend's back.

"Just a second, Rob," she told their teacher, who nodded.

"Take all the time you want," he replied. "The first trip down is always the scariest."

"You definitely can do this," JoJo said, turning to face Miley. "Remember how that one time when we were at the pool and you thought you couldn't dive into the deep end? And then you did it once, and you were never scared again? This is just like that. You just have to be brave. And Miley, you're braver than anyone I know!"

"Not as brave as you, JoJo," she said.

"Of course you are," JoJo told her friend. She desperately wanted to give Miley a hug, but they were like two giant cotton balls in their snow suits! And besides, they were holding ski poles. Then JoJo thought of something.

"Maybe you noticed something about us," she started to sing, while Rob looked on. Then JoJo pulled down her ski mask and let the bitter wind cross her face. It stung a little, but she needed Miley to hear her.

"The things we do so well," she continued, singing with all her might. "We do it
better when we're together, and everyone
can tell."

JoJo kept going, belting out the words to
"Every Girl's a Super Girl," until Miley pulled
down her own face mask and started to
sing along. Finally, they got to JoJo's favorite
chorus:

Fearless, unstoppable
Courageous, invincible
We're human, unshakable
Every girl's a super girl.

They screamed out the last line—*every*
girl's a super girl!—into the wind, at the top of
their lungs. Miley was laughing by the time
they finished singing, and JoJo could tell that
under Rob's ski mask, he was too.

"You know when I wrote that song, I was thinking of you, right?" JoJo asked Miley, who grinned big.

"JoJo, there is no one in the world who could make me feel braver than you do," she said. "I'm ready now." She turned to Rob. "Let's do this!"

"You got it, kid!" They all put their face masks back on, and Rob took both of Miley's hands in his, facing her as he skied backward, and began to guide her down the slope. JoJo followed, leaning from side-to-side in her wedge formation like Rob had taught her. She picked up her pace and enjoyed the feeling of her skis cutting through the snow, and the wind whizzing past her. Skiing was fun! She could totally get used to it, she realized.

By the time they hit the bottom of the slope, JoJo was feeling the same kind of heady excitement that she got every time she went on stage. Mrs. Lee was waiting for them at the bottom, grinning from ear-to-ear.

"That was awesome!" JoJo told her. "Seriously, so exciting. Thank you, Mrs. Lee!"

"You did it all by yourself! That's amazing, JoJo."

"Miley was super brave too," JoJo commented, high-fiving her friend. "What did you think, Miley? Were you all good the rest of the way down?"

"Yeah!" Miley exclaimed, enthusiastic. "But you know what, JoJo? I don't think I'm going to do it again. I'm so glad I gave it a try, but I think I'm more of an ice skater than a skier."

"There is a lot of courage in knowing what is right for you," Mrs. Lee told her. "You tried it, and gave it your all—I'm so proud of both you girls! What do you say we make our way over to the rink? Michelle is going to be finishing up her dress rehearsal soon and giving lessons to little kids. You're welcome to skate along with them. Or JoJo, if you like, you can do a few more runs on the ski slopes."

"Nah, maybe later. I'd rather spend time with my friends," JoJo said. It was true—she'd had a blast skiing, but nothing was more fun than being with her friends! Plus, she wanted to wear the costumes she and Miley had packed. "Can we swing up to the room for a wardrobe change?" JoJo asked. "You did say this rink is indoors, right?"

Miley grinned wide, and Mrs. Lee smiled, looking curious.

"Of course!" She said. "There's even time for hot cocoa to go!"

Back up in the room, BowBow was barking up a storm.

"What's up, cutie pie?" JoJo asked her pup. "Do you need to go outside?" BowBow stood on her hind legs and hopped around like that until JoJo grabbed her leash.

"Mrs. Lee, can I take BowBow right out front? I'll come straight back."

"Of course, sweetie. Just don't go beyond the front entrance to the resort."

"Oh, I won't," JoJo said. "It's cold out there anyway! I'll be back in five."

When JoJo stepped off the elevator with BowBow, three little kids ran up to her to *ooh* and *ahh* over BowBow. That tended to happen wherever BowBow went! She was too cute to resist.

One little girl ignored BowBow, though, and turned her adorable, round face up to JoJo. JoJo noticed she was wearing a big, rhinestone-studded bow—one of JoJo's own designs! "You're JoJo Siwa," the girl exclaimed, tugging on JoJo's arm. "You took a picture with my mommy!" Just then, the waitress from the night before—Francie—came running up.

"Abigail! Sweetie, don't tug on JoJo like that," she said, frowning lightly.

"Oh, it's okay! I love meeting fans," JoJo told her. "Abigail, I'm so glad to meet you! Your mom told me all about you. Are you on your way to go skating?"

"I sure am," Abigail told her proudly. "I can't wait to meet the *real* Snow Queen!"

"We've been reading the original story together," Francie explained. "As well as *Hans Brinker, or The Silver Skates*. Abigail is turning into a skating fanatic!"

"Well those are some great stories, Abigail," JoJo told the little girl. "And I just know my friend the Snow Queen will be so excited to meet you. I'm going to take BowBow outside now, but I'll see you over there!"

"JoJo, you are so good with kids," Francie said gratefully. "Thank you for taking the time."

"It's my pleasure," JoJo said, meaning it. Then she took BowBow outside and let her off leash in a snow-covered area on the property that was several yards from the main driveway.

Mrs. Lee hadn't been kidding! BowBow was *obsessed* with the snow!

JoJo was afraid the snow was so high BowBow would sink right through it! But she hopped in and out of it like a little rabbit, just like Michelle and her mom had said Shiny used to do. JoJo couldn't stop giggling at her happy little furball! Thank goodness for BowBow's sparkly red bow, in honor of the holidays—it made her easy to spot in all that snow.

And BowBow had made a lot of friends. Some of the little kids from Abigail's group had come outside with their parents to admire BowBow.

"That is the cutest dog *ever*," said one parent, taking a photo of BowBow.

"Just don't forget to tag her," joked JoJo. "She's at @itsbowbowsiwa on Instagram!"

"Really?" One of the kids, a little boy with glasses, looked amazed. "Is she famous?"

"Sort of," giggled JoJo. "She has a million followers!"

Then JoJo sort of wished she hadn't said it, because suddenly *everyone* was taking photos! As soon as BowBow peed, JoJo scooped her up and headed back inside.

"Sorry about that, BowBow," she said to her dog. "You just can't help how cute you are, can you?"

By the time JoJo got back upstairs to the room, Miley had already changed into JoJo's glittery red-and-white Christmas costume from her dance performance the previous year. "How do I look?" she asked her friend, twirling.

"You look almost perfect," JoJo said.

"Almost?" Miley pretend-pouted.

"You're just missing one thing." JoJo rummaged in her bag and pulled out a candy-cane-striped bow, then affixed it to her friend's curly hair. "Now you're perfect!" JoJo exclaimed.

"Girls, are you ready?" Mrs. Lee asked through the open door.

"Give me one minute," JoJo called. Then she scurried to put on her own holiday costume—the new one she was wearing that year for her Nickelodeon holiday special. It was her favorite design Nickelodeon had ever made for her! The skirt was red with white trim, and the top was red-and-white striped like a candy cane—sort of like the bow she'd given Miley. She had a green belt to wrap around her waist. And best of all, the top was super special, almost like a cowgirl costume. A green fabric panel covered her shoulders, with white beads beneath it, and a layer of white and red fringe under that. When JoJo spun, the fringe flew up in the air.

"Whoa," Miley said when she had it on. "That is *the coolest*."

"I know!" JoJo squealed. "It's literally my favorite ever and you know I love all my costumes."

"Wow!" Mrs. Lee came into the room, coat and bag in hand. "You girls look fabulous!

Michelle will get such a kick out of your festive costumes! I called a car already, so let's head downstairs. We'll rent you some ice skates when we arrive."

JoJo left BowBow a treat and made sure her dishes were filled with food and water, then followed Mrs. Lee downstairs. When they got to the lobby, they stopped at the hot cocoa bar.

"Help yourselves," Mrs. Lee encouraged. "They have to-go cups with lids!"

"And the marshmallows are red," Miley pointed out. "Don't mind if I do!"

As JoJo was pouring her cocoa from the spigot, Miley went for the marshmallows. Out of the corner of her eye, JoJo saw Miley's hand collide with someone else's. They both gripped the tongs in the marshmallow bowl, neither one willing to drop their hold.

"Hey," Miley said. "I was here first!"

"Actually, I was here first," said the owner of the competing hand. JoJo finished filling her cup and turned to watch the action unfold. Meanwhile, Mrs. Lee was on the phone to the driver of the car, letting him know which entrance they were at.

Miley let go of the tongs and put her hands on her hips. "How rude," she told the boy, who was tall and lanky with freckles and was plopping marshmallows in his cup.

"I could say the same thing," he replied. "I was in the middle of selecting my marshmallows when you tried to grab the tongs out of my hand!"

"I thought you were finished," Miley protested. "You already had one marshmallow in your cup."

"Aha!" The boy's voice was gleeful. "So you admit it, then. I *was* here first."

"Maybe," Miley said, blushing. "Fine. I admit it. I'm sorry, but we were in a rush."

As JoJo watched, she noticed that the boy had gone ahead and placed two marshmallows in Miley's cup. Then he motioned to JoJo with the tongs. "Would you like one?" he asked.

"Sure, thanks," JoJo said. "What's your name? I'm JoJo, and this is Miley."

"Hey," Miley said, staring down at her cup. "How did those . . . ? Oh," she said. "Thank you."

"No problem," the boy said. "I'm Eric. Really nice to meet you both."

JoJo noticed that although he had said, "nice to meet you both," he was looking only at Miley, who placed her cocoa back on the table and bent to re-tie her sneakers, blushing all the while. Just then, Mrs. Lee came over.

"Girls, time to go—the car's here! Oh, hello, Eric! Nice to see you!"

"Hi, Mrs. Lee. Are you heading over to the skating rink?"

"We sure are. I see you met Michelle's friends? Why aren't you over there?"

Eric held out his leg. "Twisted ankle," he said. "I can't skate this year. But I came to cheer everyone on."

"That's sweet of you," Mrs. Lee said warmly. "Then we'll see you in the stands!"

"See you there," Eric agreed.

"Bye," JoJo said, elbowing Miley, who was uncharacteristically silent.

"Bye," she mumbled. Then they piled in the back of the taxi and rode out into the afternoon snowstorm.

CHAPTER FOUR

"**E**ric is such a nice boy, isn't he? He's such a good skater too. He and Michelle have known each other for years," Mrs. Lee explained. "He'll probably go to the Olympics one day."

"I don't know, he seemed a little rude," Miley said. JoJo handed Miley her hot chocolate, and Miley took a long sip. Miley had forgotten her own at the hotel in the rush.

"Oh?" Mrs. Lee sounded confused. "Well, that doesn't sound like him." JoJo stared at her best friend, who wasn't usually so easily offended. And on top of it, Miley *loved* ice skating and she *loved* the Olympics! In fact, she'd been a huge fan of Michelle's before they'd all become friends. But she'd been quiet ever since their encounter with Eric—practically the entire way to the rink—which was unusual for a chatterbox like she was. At first JoJo had chalked it up to fear of driving in swirling snow, but now she wasn't so sure.

"Mrs. Lee, are you sure the snow is supposed to let up in time for Christmas Eve?" JoJo asked. The snow was falling as steadily as ever, and their flight home was Christmas Eve day. JoJo was starting to get worried!

"That's what the forecast says," Mrs. Lee replied. "But I agree that it isn't showing any signs of stopping. Let's just keep our fingers crossed and have fun for now. We have almost two days before we have to worry about it."

JoJo nodded. Mrs. Lee was right; all that made sense for now was to just have fun and enjoy their vacation.

"Everybody out," Mrs. Lee broke in. "Here we are!"

JoJo and Miley slid out of the car and followed Mrs. Lee into the rink. Miley's spirits seemed to rise almost immediately when she spotted Michelle through the observation deck.

"I can't wait to get out there!" she exclaimed, making JoJo smile.

"Let's get you two some ice skates," Mrs. Lee said, directing them to the front desk.

The girls gave their sizes to the man behind the counter, and then they were each handed a pair of beautiful white figure skates. Then they made their way into the rink area and sat on the bleachers, where they began to slip on their skates. Michelle spotted them and gave them a huge smile and enthusiastic wave. She knelt to say something to a child she had been helping, then skated over to the low barrier that separated the rink from the bleachers.

"You came!" she said. "I'm so glad! And you two look incredible! I love those sparkly holiday costumes!"

"Thanks!" said JoJo. She grabbed Miley's arm and the two did a twirl, showing off their festive looks.

"Of course we came, sweetie! How did dress rehearsal go?" Mrs. Lee asked.

"It was amazing!" Michelle exclaimed. "It made me so excited to perform tomorrow! I can't wait!"

"Well we can't wait to see you perform," Miley said enthusiastically. She tied the laces of her skates in double knots and stood up.

"Come on out," Michelle told them. "I've missed you two all day!"

"And we've been looking forward to this all day," JoJo exclaimed. "Haven't we, Miley?"

But Miley was already on the ice, zipping around like a pro! JoJo was proud of her BFF. Miley had fallen while ice-skating and hurt her ankle just before her birthday that year, but the second it healed she'd gone right back out and wasn't scared at all.

"You're so good!" Michelle exclaimed when she and JoJo caught up to Miley.

"I think flat surfaces are more my thing," Miley told her with a laugh.

Michelle lifted her eyebrows questioningly, but just then, little Abigail shouted her name.

Rather, she shouted, *"Snow Queen!"* Abigail and Francie were skating their way.

"Hi, cutie!" Michelle said, smiling down at the younger girl. "Are you here for a lesson?"

"I sure am!" Abigail said delightedly, letting go of her mom's hand and reaching for Michelle's. "I want to be a dancer just like you when I grow up!"

Michelle laughed. "Well from the look of it, you're already halfway there," she told Abigail. Then she held Abigail's hand high and helped her turn in a pirouette. "I'll catch up with you two later," she said to JoJo and Miley. "Promise!"

JoJo nodded. She turned to Miley, but Miley was staring at something on the opposite side of the rink with an odd expression on her face. JoJo followed Miley's gaze. There, just outside the rink, was Eric! He was giving a little boy a high-five, and a few other kids were crowded around him with notebooks and pens. *Autographs,* JoJo realized. Another boy around Eric's age was standing next to him, looking amused by the scene.

"Wow, he really is big-time!" she said to Miley, who jumped and nearly stumbled. JoJo reached out to steady her.

"Who?" Miley asked.

"Um, the guy you were just staring at? Eric, of course! What's up with you?" JoJo asked, teasingly. "You've been acting funny ever since hot cocoa!"

"I don't know what you're talking about," Miley said stiffly, then zipped away from JoJo and started to circle the rink.

JoJo stared after her best friend, hurt. What had she done to offend Miley? *Maybe it was the skiing,* she thought. Maybe Miley was feeling a little embarrassed about getting scared, when usually she was so bold and brave. JoJo hoped not. There was nothing wrong with feeling scared sometimes! And that was the whole point of friends—to lean on when you were feeling bad, and to do the same for them. JoJo bit her lip. She hoped Miley wasn't shutting her out.

With all the snow that made her worried about getting home for Christmas—and with Miley shutting her out—JoJo felt like their fun adventure was turning into more than she'd bargained for. All of a sudden, JoJo missed her mom, who gave the *best* advice. She resolved to call her the second she had some down time.

Back in the resort that night, the snow was still showing no sign of letting up.

"This is wild!" exclaimed Mrs. Lee. "Michelle, I just got word that the show is officially in the rink where you practiced today, rather than the outdoor rink at the resort. That is, *if* the roads stay open."

"Oh no! Is there a chance it might be canceled altogether?" Michelle wanted to know. She was lying on her bed and idly flipping through TV channels.

"It doesn't look like it, but there may not be as many people there as last year, due to the weather. Girls, I'm afraid the weather reports have changed. Tomorrow, the storm is supposed to pick up. There is a very small chance it'll affect our flight home on Thursday."

JoJo's heart sank. She loved Christmas Eve with her family. They ate all their favorite foods and exchanged silly gifts and goofed around and watched Christmas movies. Worse, if they didn't make it home on Christmas Eve, that meant she wouldn't wake up in her own bed on Christmas morning.

"I think I'll call my mom," she told Mrs. Lee. "I've only texted with her since we arrived, and I want to let her know what's going on."

"Of course," Mrs. Lee said. "Do you want to go into my room for privacy?"

JoJo smiled gratefully and nodded. Then she took her phone into Mrs. Lee's room, closed the door, and dialed her mom on FaceTime.

"Hey, kiddo!" Her mom said when she picked up. "Are you having a good time?"

"Yes!" The sight of her mom's face made JoJo feel instantly better. "I went skiing for the first time this morning, and ice-skating this afternoon. It was so fun! And Mom, you should see this place—it's so cool. It's really pretty, and there's a skating rink just outside. Although it's too snowy to really go out there right now . . . actually we might go to the indoor pool later on and have relay races! Mrs. Lee is so nice, and our beds are super comfy. And we haven't even explored town yet! There's supposedly this really amazing ice cream shop . . ."

"Whoa, whoa, slow down! Ice cream in the snow? Are you for real?" JoJo's mom was laughing. "I'm glad you're having such a good time, honey. I can't wait to see you in a couple of days, though! We all miss you and BowBow."

"We sure do," said JoJo's dad, popping in the frame as he strolled through the kitchen. JoJo's mom followed him with the phone.

"Hi, Dad!" JoJo waved, and he blew her a kiss before dipping into the fridge for a snack. "Mom," JoJo said, "that's actually what I wanted to talk to you about. Have you seen the weather reports for up north? It's been snowing hard. I mean, I don't know what it's like to be in a blizzard but it sure looks like one. I can hardly see out the hotel window right now! I'm worried our flight will be canceled and I won't make it home for Christmas. And on top of it"—JoJo lowered her voice—"I think Miley's mad at me, or something."

"Slow down," her mom said. "One thing at a time. First of all, you and Miley have never had an issue you couldn't resolve. Did something happen?"

"No . . ." JoJo trailed off. "Well, not exactly. She didn't have very much fun on the slopes.

She got scared. And she was a little rude to a boy we met at the hot cocoa. And since then she just hasn't been herself."

"Sweetheart," her mom said. "It's important to remember that this probably isn't about you at all. Give Miley a little time and space. She'll open up to you when she's ready. Being a good friend means listening when that time comes. I know Miley, and I know how much she loves you. I'm willing to bet Miley doesn't even know she's been acting funny. Maybe she's just figuring something out that she isn't ready to share just yet."

"But we tell each other everything!" JoJo protested.

"Yes," her mom said carefully. "That's true. But Miley may not even know what's bothering her—assuming something is. She might need some time to explore her feelings before she understands them and *can* share them with you. Make sense?"

"Yes, I think so," JoJo said.

"The best thing to do now is just be the sweet, fun friend you always are. Miley will come around."

"Thanks, Mom. I miss you," JoJo told her. She felt her throat tighten a little. She really, *really* wanted to be home for the holidays, but she also knew there was nothing she could do to control the weather, and she was lucky to be having so much fun.

"Miss you too, JoJo." JoJo felt her heart fill up. "And don't worry about Christmas. Christmas is all about the people you're with, not the day itself—so it'll happen whenever you get home. Just have a good time with your friends and we'll see you soon." Her mom sent her an air kiss and waved goodbye.

After they hung up, JoJo headed back into the big rec room with the foosball table. Michelle and Miley were sprawled out on the sofa eating pizza and putting together a puzzle, and Mrs. Lee was reading a book and drinking tea.

"There she is!" she said, looking up from her book as JoJo walked in. "Did you connect with your mom?"

"Yep!" JoJo walked over to the pizza box and grabbed a slice.

"We missed you!" said Miley, and instantly JoJo felt better. She settled in between her friends and took a look at the puzzle. Then she reached in the pile of pieces and found a perfect fit.

"Girl, we've been staring at this puzzle for ten minutes!" Michelle exclaimed. "How did you do that?"

JoJo shrugged. "I do puzzles with my mom all the time," she said. "It's kind of our thing." She tucked her feet underneath her and chomped into the cheesy, yummy pizza, then clicked two other puzzle pieces into place.

Miley squealed delightedly and Michelle shook her head, grinning. It was hard being away from family, JoJo realized, but her friends were basically her second family. Her mom was right—it was all about the people you were with.

JoJo finished the last bite of her pizza and wiped off her fingers. Then she tackle-hugged Miley and Michelle, who were sitting next to each other.

"Hey!" Miley said. "Lay off!" but she was giggling.

"Give a girl some space," Michelle called out dramatically, in between laughter. BowBow jumped around them, barking and hopping up and down.

Mrs. Lee shook her head. "You girls are truly special," she told them. "You're a lucky bunch."

JoJo couldn't have agreed more.

CHAPTER FIVE

"**M**iley," JoJo said the next morning. "Wake up!"

Usually JoJo loved sleeping in, but when she woke up that morning, all she could think about was how much they had yet to explore! It was their last day at the resort, and the day of Michelle's big performance. But they had the whole morning free before it was due to start.

"JoJo, it's so early," Miley protested, rubbing sleep from her eyes.

"It is not," JoJo told her. "Miley, it's nine o'clock! Michelle left a while ago. This is our very last day! I want to explore the indoor pool, and don't you want to play in the snow?"

"I do . . ." Miley said. "But I also need my beauty rest."

"Beauty rest patootie rest," JoJo scoffed. "BowBow needs to go for a walk. Why don't you come with?"

After Miley finally dragged herself out of bed, the girls let Mrs. Lee know they were going downstairs to take BowBow out. On their way out, they ran into Eric, who was helping himself to hot cocoa with a friend.

"Hot cocoa for breakfast?" Miley asked, curling her lip. "So gross. Your teeth are going to rot!"

94

"Miley!" JoJo exclaimed, surprised. But instead of responding, Miley just grabbed BowBow's leash from JoJo and walked outside, her nose in the air.

"I don't think she likes me much," Eric said, looking a little hurt.

"I don't think that's true," JoJo said, although she wasn't 100 percent sure. "And anyway, I say any time of day is a good time for hot cocoa!"

Eric brightened. "JoJo, this is my friend Theodore," he said, introducing a boy around JoJo's height with curly hair, who was dressed in a red T-shirt and sneakers. Eric's own shoes were light-up hightops.

"Cool shoes," JoJo told Eric appreciatively.

"Thanks!" he said. "I got them for Hanukkah."

"Cool!" JoJo exclaimed. She was curious to ask Eric more about Hanukkah, but just then Theodore interjected.

"I celebrate two holidays," he told them. "Christmas on my mom's side, and my dad's side celebrates Kwanzaa. We'll be doing that next week."

"What's Kwanzaa?" JoJo asked. A holiday she'd never even heard of was interesting too! Theodore opened his mouth to reply, but just then, BowBow bounded back in, her leash dragging behind her, and Theodore bent to pet the dog. Miley followed, out of breath.

JoJo was curious to ask both Eric and Theodore more about their holiday traditions, but it would have to wait.

"I'm sorry, JoJo," Miley said, as BowBow rolled onto her back, dripping melting snow all over the tile floor. "I dropped the leash, and she just took off!"

JoJo wasn't thrilled about that, but she knew it was an accident; and anyway, Bow-Bow was clearly safe and sound, thank goodness.

"It's okay," she told her friend. "But next time wait for me, all right? I don't want Bow-Bow to get lost outside."

"You're lucky she ran right back in here," Eric chimed in. "My dog would have run for the hills!" He crouched down to give Bow-Bow a scratch behind the ears. "Good girl, running back to your mom!" he said, congratulating BowBow, who offered him a paw in return.

Miley was silent. Then her face darkened.

Uh-oh, thought JoJo. It was as if a storm cloud had passed over her friend's face!

"I'm going back upstairs," she said stiffly. "Didn't you want to go swimming, JoJo?"

"Oh cool, are you guys trying out the indoor pool?" Eric chimed in. "Maybe we'll tag along! Theo, you've been wanting to check it out, right?"

Theodore nodded. "There's supposedly a water slide," he said.

"That's okay. We need some alone time," Miley said, her voice crisp.

"Well, I mean, anyone can use the pool," JoJo tried, keeping her voice neutral. "The more the merrier, right? Anyway, we're going upstairs to grab our suits. Theodore, I want to hear more about Kwanzaa later— I'm super curious, since I don't know anything about it. See you guys around!" She gave their new friends an extra sunny smile to make up for Miley's receding back—she'd walked away without saying goodbye and was already at the elevator bank! JoJo dashed after her with BowBow in her arms.

"Miley," she said, once they were alone in the elevator. "What is going on? You usually love making new friends."

"Nothing," Miley mumbled, avoiding JoJo's gaze. "I just didn't like them."

"But Miley, we're Siwanatorz," JoJo pointed out. "We always give other people a chance. Those boys seemed really nice. And Theodore was telling me about his family's holiday traditions."

"Mrs. Lee would have worried if we were gone much longer," Miley told her.

She had a point, so JoJo let it go. She remembered what her mom said: Miley would open up to her when she was ready. But boy, JoJo hoped that would be soon! Moody Miley was wearing her thin!

99

After their swim—Theodore had been right, there *was* a water slide, and a twisty one at that!—and a lunch of sandwiches with Mrs. Lee in the lobby, the girls got cleaned up and donned their holiday costumes again.

"They're cute," JoJo said with a shrug. "Why not wear them as much as we can?"

"I agree," Miley told her. They'd had a blast in the pool, doing handstand contests and backflips off the diving board and going down the slide at least a dozen times. Miley was back to her normal, cheerful self. "They're way too festive and sparkly to waste."

"How about different accessories, though?" JoJo said, opening her suitcase to reveal her bow collection. "I'm thinking I could use a pop of red with my red." She giggled.

"Maybe I'll do blue for Hanukkah," Miley suggested.

"Hanukkah?" JoJo furrowed her brow. "But you don't celebrate Hanukkah."

"I just thought it would be nice to celebrate all the holidays happening now," Miley said. But she looked embarrassed, and returned the bow to the bag, swapping it out for a silver one. "Never mind, this one is better anyway."

"Miley," JoJo said, her voice gentle. "Are you okay? You've been acting kind of funny lately."

"I'm fine, JoJo!" Miley exclaimed. "Geez."

"Okay," JoJo said doubtfully. She clipped her own bow—a red one that reminded her of a Christmas ornament—onto her side ponytail, and tried not to let Miley's words sting. After all, it was Christmas week! And

101

JoJo was determined to be full of holiday spirit.

The drive to the rink was even whiter and more blizzard-y than the last. Even Mrs. Lee looked a little worried as the driver navigated the car along slippery roads for the five-minute journey.

"I'm glad it's so close," she remarked. "But I'd be surprised if many people turned out on an afternoon like this one."

Still, there was a good crowd in the rink's bleachers. And when the lights began to dim and music played, JoJo forgot all about the weather—she and Miley were both sitting on the edges of their seats with excitement, eager to see Michelle perform.

When spotlights hit the ice, illuminating Michelle as the Snow Queen, JoJo let out a gasp. Their friend was *gorgeous* in a glittery, blue-and-white dress, a faux-fur lined cape, and a towering tiara that looked as if it were made of icicles. As Michelle moved along the ice, she was so graceful she appeared to float. Her costume billowed behind her, highlighting the scene's dramatic effect. JoJo was mesmerized.

Throughout the entire hour-and-a-half show, JoJo only removed her eyes from Michelle once, to look at Miley. Miley was rapt, leaning forward with her elbows balanced on her knees and her chin propped on her hands. Her long, curly hair partially obscured her face, but JoJo could see her eyes, and they were bright with wonder. JoJo knew she was drinking in the choreography, probably even taking mental notes.

When it was over, Michelle slid into her final pose and bowed her head, and the lights dimmed again. There was a long silence. Then the audience burst into applause.

When the spotlight came back on, Michelle was standing with her castmates. Together, they clasped hands, and they all took a bow. Everyone in the audience whistled and cheered, and some people even called for an encore! Rose petals floated from somewhere higher in the stands and landed on the ice. JoJo beamed—she could not have been more proud!

You were incredible," JoJo squealed, wrapping Michelle in a hug a few minutes later.

"I couldn't agree more," Mrs. Lee said, giving Michelle a peck on the cheek. "You were incandescent, sweetie."

"Oh, Mom." But Michelle was blushing.

"You nailed it," Miley agreed. "And who was your choreographer? That final sequence at the end was so complicated, but you made it look so simple! I wish I could pick their brain," Miley said, sighing. "I bet I'd learn a lot!"

"You can," Michelle told her. "I'll introduce you when we're back in LA sometime. She lives there too. She's mega talented."

"I'll say." Miley and Michelle nerded out over choreography the entire way out of the rink. But when they reached the front door, they all stopped cold.

It had snowed another *foot*, at least, since they'd been inside—and the snow was so heavy that JoJo could hardly even see the shuttles lined up to take them back to Tinseltown—a courtesy from the hotel due to all the snow.

"Well," said Mrs. Lee briskly. "I'm sure they've been plowing the roads, anyway. Let's get back to the resort before it gets any worse."

They piled into the shuttle and buckled up.

"How are the driving conditions?" Mrs. Lee asked the driver.

"Better than you'd think," the driver told her. "But this is my last trip for the night. It's supposed to get even worse over the next few hours, if you can believe it." He pulled out of the parking lot and carefully navigated the car onto the road. "Yep, I'm just going to get home before the roads close altogether."

Miley and JoJo exchanged a look, and Michelle bit her lip. JoJo noticed that Miley's left hand was gripping the door handle hard, so hard her knuckles were turning white.

"Almost there," JoJo assured her. Miley pressed her lips together in a thin line.

Mrs. Lee looked worried too.

"Girls," she said, as they finally pulled into the cul-de-sac at the resort entrance. "If it keeps up like this, our 7 A.M. flight might get canceled. And if that happens, we will just have to have an amazing holiday right here at the resort."

"Okay," JoJo said, trying to sound positive. But her heart sank. She'd never in her life not spent Christmas Eve and Christmas day with her mom, dad, and brother.

They went straight to the resort restaurant for an early dinner.

"Wow," Michelle said when they got settled in their seats. "It's a complete whiteout! You can't even see the rink or the mountains anymore."

"It's pretty cool," Miley said, her voice filled with awe. "I can't believe I'd never seen snow, and now I'm seeing a blizzard!"

Mrs. Lee was on the phone with the airlines, checking their flight for the next morning. When she hung up, her face was grim.

"So far, so good," she said. "But I checked the weather report too, and the storm isn't showing any sign of letting up. We'll have to keep an eye on the weather and check again first thing in the morning. But for now, let's enjoy a cozy time here. I looked at the activity schedule earlier, and there are games in the lobby tonight. How about a nice dinner, followed by dessert and game night?"

JoJo cheered along with Miley and Michelle, but she felt a small pang of worry. It was a strange feeling, to have so much fun with her friends but also want to be somewhere else!

Game night turned out to be bingo. It was supervised by hotel staff, so Mrs. Lee went upstairs to relax and touch base with Michelle's dad and little sister while the kids were downstairs. Michelle won a giant chocolate bar, and Miley won a set of beaded bracelets.

"Hey! How come I didn't win anything?" JoJo asked, hands on her hips.

"You're always a winner in my book," Miley chuckled. "But here, you can share my bracelet prize!" She slid one of the beaded bracelets off her wrist and handed it to JoJo.

"Thanks, pal," JoJo said. She was glad Miley was being herself again!

"And we can all share my chocolate," Michelle put in.

"I hope so! That thing is as big as your head!" JoJo and Miley giggled.

Just then, Eric and Theodore strolled over. Eric was wearing a Tinseltown baseball cap that he won at bingo.

"Hi!" JoJo said, waving at the boys. "Nice cap!"

"Thanks, JoJo," Eric said. "Michelle, you were amazing today in *The Snow Queen on Ice!* Both of us were there, and we loved it. I only wished I could have been out there on the ice with you."

"We definitely missed you out there!" Michelle told him. "That's really sweet of you to say, though. I'm so glad you guys came to watch."

"Wouldn't have missed it," Theodore said.

"Are you a skater too?" Miley wanted to know.

"Nope, I'm a musician," Theodore told her. "I play the piano."

"Cool!" JoJo exclaimed. "There's a piano in the restaurant—maybe you can play for us!"

"Oh, I don't know." Theodore shrugged, looking bashful. "I'm not crazy about playing in front of audiences."

111

"Come on," Eric said, giving Theodore a gentle nudge. "It would be fun! Theo's so talented," he remarked to the girls. Then he turned back to Theodore. "In my opinion, you should show off a little more!"

"Nah," Theodore said, blushing. "It's really just something I do for myself."

"I get that," Miley told him. "I'm a choreographer, and sometimes it's nice to be more behind the scenes than front and center."

"What style of dance do you typically do choreography for, Miley?" Eric asked, genuinely curious. "I really admire our ice-dancing choreographers. It isn't an easy job."

Miley looked at her shoes. "All kinds," she muttered.

JoJo shot her a glance. "Miley's very talented," she told the boys. "She's choreographed a bunch of my shows."

"That is so cool!" Eric exclaimed. Theodore also looked impressed.

"It's no big deal, JoJo," Miley said.

"Where are you guys from?" JoJo asked, changing the subject.

"We're both from Tahoe," Theodore replied. "We've been friends since kindergarten! I come to Tinseltown every year with Eric to hit the slopes and see him perform."

"And we figured we wouldn't break tradition this year just because of my ankle," Eric explained.

"That's so nice," JoJo replied. "I was just thinking about tradition! Well, my family's traditions for Christmas, anyway. We're supposed to fly back to Los Angeles early tomorrow in plenty of time for Christmas Eve, but with the snow coming down the way it is, it's looking iffy."

"Same here," Theodore told them. "To Tahoe, I mean. Kwanzaa doesn't start until the day after Christmas, so I have some time to get home for that part of my family's celebration. But I'd hate to miss Christmas! Although . . ." He paused, remembering. "Once I was in the hospital with appendicitis over Kwanzaa, and at first I was really sad to miss the holiday. But then my family brought the holiday to me! Sure, we didn't plan to be in a hospital room. But looking back now, it's one of my favorite memories. Sometimes the unexpected things work out even better in the end, if you go with the flow."

"I like that," JoJo said thoughtfully. "What are you guys up to the rest of the night? We don't have plans and—"

"JoJo," Miley interrupted. "Remember that thing we have to do upstairs?"

"What?" JoJo looked at Michelle, and Michelle only shrugged, as confused as JoJo was.

"We have to walk BowBow," Miley said, her voice firm.

"Michelle's mom walked BowBow while we were playing bingo," JoJo protested. "And it's only seven o'clock. Do you really want to go back to the room already?"

"Yeah," Eric weighed in. "Miley, I'd really love to hear more about your choreography! We could even just play cards by the fire, or something," he suggested, suddenly looking shy.

"No, thanks." Miley swiveled on her heel and walked at a fast clip toward the elevators. "Aren't you coming?" she said over her should to JoJo and Michelle.

"I guess we are," Michelle said lightly. "See you later, guys! Maybe we'll catch up with you more tomorrow morning."

"Bye!" JoJo said brightly, waving to both boys. She wanted to give Miley the benefit of the doubt, but she was having trouble understanding her friend's unfriendly behavior. It wasn't their typical, fun-loving, sweet and sunny Miley! JoJo remembered her mom's advice—to wait. But JoJo wondered if by storming off, Miley was sending her the message that she needed to talk.

"Hey," she said, when all three girls were back in the hotel room and sitting cross-legged in their pajamas on one of the big beds. "Are you okay, Miley?"

"Yeah." Michelle looked concerned. "You seem a little upset. We're here for you, Miley! If something's wrong, you can tell us."

To JoJo's surprise, Miley burst into tears.

"Miley!" JoJo wrapped her arms around her friend. "What's the matter?"

Miley sniffled, and Michelle hopped off the bed and went to the bathroom, returning with a box of tissues.

"I feel so silly," Miley started.

"It's okay, whatever it is." JoJo scooted closer to Miley and kept one arm around her shoulders while Miley began to talk.

"It's just . . . ," she began, taking a breath and dabbing at her eyes with her tissue. "It's that guy, Eric."

"Yeah, I can tell you don't like him very much," JoJo said carefully. "I'm just not sure why."

"That's the thing," Miley told her. "I do like him. I think I . . . *like* like him." She buried her face in her hands.

"Oh!" said Michelle, a smile spreading across her face.

"Oh," JoJo said, stunned. Neither she nor Miley had ever had a crush before, until now.

"I'm so embarrassed," Miley said. Her voice was muffled under her hands. "It's just, I get flutters when I'm around him and I don't know how to act."

"That's completely normal," Michelle said, rubbing Miley's back. "I did the exact same thing when I had my first crush. Whenever he said 'hi,' I looked at the ground and ran away!" JoJo look at Michelle with curiosity—Michelle was a few years older than JoJo and Miley, but JoJo hadn't really ever thought about her having crushes. JoJo knew her parents had crushes on each other, and she knew someday she'd probably have a crush on someone too. Usually she and Miley went through all the same things at the same time—they were BFFs, after all! But in this case, JoJo was glad Michelle was around to help Miley.

"What do I do?" Miley asked, looking up at Michelle.

"Well," Michelle said, smiling, "you just say hi and talk like you do with any other person."

"But it's so scary," Miley protested.

"But you're brave," Michelle reminded her.

Miley shook her head. She sniffled. "I'm not sure I am," she admitted. "It's just, JoJo, you're so brave. And Michelle, you too. You're both used to performing in front of big crowds, and doing scary things. JoJo, when we had our ski lesson the other day, you just went for it. And I was the one who almost didn't make it. I'm the behind-the-scenes girl, not the girl in the spotlight."

"Oh, Miley! You have no idea how bright you shine," JoJo told her friend. She was starting to get a little choked up too. "You don't have to be center stage to sparkle," she added. "You are one of the best choreographers I've ever met. And that includes all the grown-up choreographers I work with on my shows."

"And you are an incredible skater," Michelle added. "Miley, you could probably do that professionally if you wanted!"

"It's true," JoJo said. "You looked so comfortable on the ice. And for me, *that's* scary! And when we were skiing, you did make it down. That's what counts. Bravery is about being strong when things are scary—not about not being scared at all."

"Besides, everyone gets scared sometimes. And the things you've been scared of this week, well—they're new! You had never skied before. You'd never even seen snow," Michelle pointed out, "practically until you were coasting down a hill covered in it. And you've never had a crush on someone until now, right?"

Miley nodded. She blew her nose and wiped her eyes with the sleeve of her pajama top. She squeezed JoJo tight, then hugged Michelle as well.

"You're right," she said. "I *am* brave. And I *do* sparkle. There is more than one way to sparkle."

"Yeah!" JoJo and Michelle cheered.

"I feel so much better," Miley told them. "You guys are the best. But there's just one problem."

"What's that?" Michelle wanted to know.

"I won't get my chance to be brave with Eric! We're leaving tomorrow morning."

"I wouldn't be so sure of that," Mrs. Lee said, entering the room in her slippers and robe. "Girls," she said. "I have disappointing news. All flights leaving the airport tomorrow morning are canceled."

"Could we take a later flight?" JoJo asked hopefully.

"Unfortunately, as of right now the airport is closed tomorrow. We're rebooked on a flight leaving early Christmas day. I just called your parents to let them know. I'm so sorry. I know how badly you all wanted to be home on Christmas Eve."

The three girls exchanged mischievous looks.

"I don't know," JoJo said, a grin crossing her features. "Suddenly a little more time at the resort isn't looking so bad!"

CHAPTER SIX

The next morning, the girls hatched a plan.

"First we check in with our parents," said JoJo through a mouthful of waffles. "Then we have a snowball fight. Then Miley talks to Eric."

"I'm not sure how that will happen," Miley told her doubtfully, cutting into her omelet. They had gotten room service—*again*—

because they'd decided eating in their pjs was their very favorite thing. "Maybe Eric and Theodore went home already."

"They couldn't have!" JoJo exclaimed. "You heard them—they had a flight out to Tahoe this morning. But the airport is closed."

"Oh, right." Miley looked hopeful. Then her face fell. "Is this silly?" she asked.

"Not at all," said Michelle. "I know Eric personally, and he's really nice. Worst case, you make a new friend," she said with a shrug. "And a really cool, talented one at that."

"Guys, I have an idea." JoJo's brain had been churning while her friends talked. "Remember how Eric mentioned Hanukkah, and Theodore was talking about his family's Kwanzaa traditions?"

Her friends nodded.

"Well . . . call me crazy, but . . . aren't we all a little mopey about missing Christmas

Eve and Christmas morning with our families? Even you, Michelle. I know you miss your dad and sister, even though your mom is here."

"Totally," Michelle said, looking wistful. "It's weird to be away from home at Christmas."

"Okay, well. We're all snowbound, right? Everyone here is in the same boat. I say we make a list of our holiday traditions. Then we go down to the lobby and do a little sleuthing—find out other people's holiday traditions. Including Eric's and Theodore's," she said, giving Miley a wink. "And then we throw a huge party celebrating everyone's holidays!"

"JoJo, I love the way your mind works," Miley said, her mouth full of strawberries and whipped cream. JoJo giggled at her friend.

"What do you think, Michelle?"

"I think we should cap off the party with a late-night swim!" Michelle said. "JoJo, you're totally bringing the Christmas spirit we've been needing. Let's just talk to my mom about it—if we're throwing a lobby party, we may need to get the Tinseltown staff to okay it."

The resort staff were more than okay with JoJo's idea—they said they'd be willing to help however they could! That included providing treats and free accommodations to all stranded guests, as well as helping the girls host their impromptu holiday party that evening. For now, JoJo and her friends had set aside their snowball fight in favor of interviewing the guests who were hanging out and sipping cocoa in the lobby.

They split up and made their rounds.

JoJo spoke with four guests who had celebrated Diwali in November. Diwali was a Hindu festival of lights, to mark the victory of good over evil.

"We light oil lamps all around our house to welcome the goddess Lakshmi," said a friendly woman who was a little younger than JoJo's mom, and was running around after a set of twin toddlers. "The whole thing lasts five days, and we also use colorful sand and dried flowers to make patterns. And my kids love the sweet treats!"

When JoJo compared notes with her friends, she noticed:

❋ Miley had interviewed Eric—a big step for her!—who said his favorite Hanukkah tradition was making latkes—or potato pancakes—fried in duck fat with his mom and dad.

"Usually we have a big party for adults and kids on Hanukkah Eve," he explained. "It's my favorite thing to eat latkes and hang out with my friends and fall asleep watching movies."

✳ Eric asked Theodore to share his Kwanzaa tradition of Kuumba—creativity—with the rest of group by playing the piano. Theodore agreed as long as he could play a few Christmas carols and share his recipe for curried chicken and banana soup, his very favorite Kwanzaa meal.

✳ Even though the holidays were very different, there were some things that were the same:

❋ Everyone liked laughing on their holiday.

❀ Everyone liked being with family and friends on their holiday.

❀ Everyone had delicious treats they liked to share on their holiday.

❀ Everyone celebrated their holiday with love and togetherness.

"Well," Miley said, closing her notebook and sticking her pen behind her ear. "I think we've done some good detective work. This party is going to include something special for everyone here."

"I think you're right," Michelle agreed. "But I'm going to stay away from the food part of the party—I'm not a very good cook. I could probably find a way to burn ice cream if you let me!"

"Miley, I noticed that when you talked to Eric as an interview, you didn't look nervous at all," JoJo said. "You are amazing! Are you still feeling butterflies?"

Miley nodded, her eyes shining. "I am," she confirmed. "Even more than before. But asking Eric questions about his life took some of the pressure off, and let me relax and get to know him."

"Are you feeling like your brave self now?"

Miley grinned. "Braver than I've ever been," she said. "You were right, JoJo. I had it in me all along."

As the day went on, JoJo focused on decorations, while Michelle focused on music for the party, and Miley focused on food. The boys helped by making flyers advertising the party ("Starting at 5 P.M. sharp!") to hang around the resort.

With staff permission, JoJo took popcorn from the kitchen and invited a half dozen younger girls to help her string popcorn kernels on thread from the hotel's first aid kits. By the time they were done, they had enough popcorn garlands to wrap around the entire restaurant.

With the help of the hotel staff, JoJo also set up tables for each tradition, with special centerpieces. One table featured a grouping of nine candles to represent a menorah; one featured a homemade kinara; one was adorned with a nest of colored lights; and the last included flower petals from arrangements the hotel had replaced that morning. "They aren't dried, but I approve," the woman whom JoJo had spoken with about Diwali said with a laugh. "Sometimes we have to make do as best we can—and that looks beautiful."

Then JoJo asked the woman, whose name was Prisha, if she wouldn't mind filling out an index card with information about her holiday, to place on the table.

"I'd be happy to!" Prisha said. "What a good idea." JoJo made a mental note to ask Eric and Theodore to do the same for their holidays. She and Miley could handle Christmas.

Miley and Eric and Theodore teamed up to make Theodore's favorite Kwanzaa meal: curried chicken and banana soup. Miley sliced the banana while one of the kitchen chefs looked on to make sure Eric and Theodore were measuring the curry powder correctly and sprinkling the dish with unsweetened coconut.

Michelle made a playlist full of everyone's favorite holiday jams, and Theodore promised to play "All I Want for Christmas" on the piano, so everyone could sing along. All the kids helped the resort staff mix yummy sugar cookie batter for cut-out cookies—JoJo's favorite tradition—and put them in the oven.

While the cookies were baking, JoJo and her friends went outside.

Soon Miley was laughing with Theodore and Eric as they rolled snowballs into snow-men. (She threw one of the smaller and softer snowballs at Eric, who fell over dra-matically into a pile of snow.)

"I want to make a snow fort," JoJo told Michelle. "I've never been around enough snow to do a really cool fort, until now."

"You got it," Michelle said, packing snow in her hands. "By the way, I think our girl is having a blast." She nodded toward Miley, who was adding twig arms to her snowman.

"She sure is," JoJo agreed. "I'm proud of her for taking chances."

By the time JoJo and Michelle were done with their fort, it was practically a snow *palace.* It had a turret, a balcony you could step out on, and a tiny moat surrounding it, which Michelle had filled with water in hopes it would turn into a mini ice rink.

"This is *so cool,*" Miley said joining them. "You guys! I've never seen anything like this fort!"

It was true. JoJo looked at Michelle, who beamed back at her.

"You know what?" JoJo said to Michelle. "I miss my family, but there are no other friends I'd rather be stranded on the slopes with."

"Me too," Miley agreed. "But, brrr! I'm freezing, all of a sudden! Can we go in by the fire?"

The girls warmed up by the hearth and decorated cookies—for the second time that holiday season, but JoJo didn't mind. She would never get sick of her favorite traditions. And lots of parents brought their kids to the party! They were surrounded by kids smeared with frosting. Sprinkles were everywhere! But everyone was having *fun*.

After cookies, the resort staff brought out sliders and pizza, and everyone took a seat at the decorated holiday tables. "Dessert first on the holidays!" Francie exclaimed. "You kids really saved the day!" Then came the latkes and curried chicken soup, which everyone slurped up enthusiastically. They were full and happy when Theodore took his spot at the piano and began playing Christmas carols.

JoJo, Miley, Michelle, Mrs. Lee, Eric, and the other guests gathered around the piano. They sang their hearts out when Theodore played "All I Want for Christmas." And they went wild when Theodore transitioned into "Santa Baby" and then to "Jingle Bell Rock."

"I thought he didn't like being center stage," Michelle whispered to JoJo.

"I think he's being a good sport because he knows it makes us happy!" JoJo said, smiling. "But I also think he's having fun. Hey, you know what would make this even more fun?" JoJo said. "If BowBow were here!"

With Mrs. Lee's permission, JoJo went upstairs to their room to fetch BowBow, who was so excited to see her that she immediately gave her sloppy kisses all over. JoJo had a special Christmas outfit for Bow-Bow. She couldn't wait to see everyone's reactions! She reached into her suitcase and retrieved a miniature dog outfit, then helped her wriggly pup into it. As she was shutting the suitcase, she caught a glimpse of her bow collection. Then she had another big idea.

"**O**h my gosh, she is so cute!" little Abigail squealed at the sight of BowBow. "A teeny-tiny doggie elf!" JoJo laughed as other kids crowded around BowBow, who was indeed wearing a small green elf suit and an elf hat. JoJo wouldn't ask BowBow to wear an outfit if BowBow didn't love it! JoJo put the small dog on the ground and she immediately preened for all the kids, who gave her ear scratchies.

"I have a present for all of you," JoJo said, reaching into the tote bag she'd filled with bows before leaving the room. "Just call me Miss Claus!" JoJo had made sure there were enough bows for all the kids in attendance at the party—and she'd selected bows in colors to honor all the holidays they were celebrating. Now those kids reached in her bag and helped themselves to sparkly bows

137

in green, red, blue, white, black, silver, and gold! JoJo helped the girls and boys put them on their hair or their clothes.

"Now everyone looks ready for a party!" she exclaimed. Then she and BowBow headed back over to the piano, where Theodore was just finishing up the singalong with JoJo's friends and some of the grown-ups.

"All right, everybody!" JoJo shouted, when Theodore was done. "How about a dance party?!"

Everyone cheered as JoJo belted out her rendition of "Rocking Around the Christmas Tree." JoJo and Miley broke into a simple dance that Miley had choreographed, and soon everyone at the party was learning the steps and dancing right alongside them.

"Best party ever," JoJo cheered, when they were finished. Then she turned to Miley and

Michelle. "The only things missing are our families."

"Well, that's what FaceTime is for," Michelle pointed out. "Let's call everyone right now!" They did just that, waving and saying hi to each other's parents and siblings. JoJo loved her friends' families as if they were extensions of her own. When JoJo was wrapping up her call to her parents and brother and the party was beginning to dwindle, she realized Miley had disappeared.

"Gotta go, Mom and Dad! See you tomorrow," JoJo said.

"See you for Christmas," her mom told her.

"Love you, JoJo," said her dad.

"Love you more!"

JoJo hung up the phone and turned to Michelle, who was curled up next to her mom in front of the hearth, with BowBow at their feet. "Have you two seen Miley?" JoJo asked.

Mrs. Lee nodded. "She's over by the restaurant," she said.

JoJo tiptoed over to the hall and peeked around the corner. Then she slapped a palm over her mouth to prevent her from squealing out loud. Miley and Eric were standing at the entrance to the restaurant . . . right under the mistletoe. They were smiling and talking, and Eric was holding Miley's hand. Miley smiled up at him, her cheeks pink. JoJo hadn't seen her friend looking so happy in days!

Then Eric bent and gave Miley a sweet kiss on the cheek.

JoJo ducked back into the lounge and gave Michelle a high-five. "This Christmas Eve is *awesome*," she said.

"Girls, I am so proud of you for the way you brought holiday spirit to a situation that could have been disappointing," Mrs. Lee told them. "With kindness and creativity and a positive attitude, you really can do anything. Throwing a party together isn't easy, and you three brought lots of joy to a bunch of people tonight."

"You know what they say," JoJo joked. "It's not hard work if you love it!"

"And it's never work when we're together," Michelle chimed in.

"I couldn't agree more," JoJo told her, just as Miley returned to the lounge area, looking starry eyed.

"On *that* note," JoJo said, laughing. "Who wants to go for a late-night swim before we call it a night?"

"Me!" said Michelle.

"Me too!" said Miley.

"Me three!" said Mrs. Lee. "That is, if grown-ups are invited."

"Mrs. Lee, you're one of the gang," JoJo told her.

They went upstairs to change into their suits, and then JoJo and her friends ended the night with a splash.

CHAPTER SEVEN

"**P**lease put your tray tables in the upright position and your carry-on items under the seat in front of you," the voice intoned, as JoJo, Miley, Michelle, and Mrs. Lee got settled on their flight home, early Christmas morning. "Buckle up, and have a very merry Christmas!"

"You good?" JoJo asked Miley, remembering how scared she was on the flight to

Tinseltown. JoJo offered her palm, in case Miley wanted to squeeze it for take-off.

But instead of accepting JoJo's hand, Miley gave her a casual thumbs-up, then returned to filtering through the movie selection. "You want to watch a movie together?" she asked. JoJo smiled. Miley sometimes got scared, but she conquered her fears just as soon as she felt them.

"I sure do," JoJo said. "What about *The Grinch*? I've never seen it, if you can believe it."

"Whaaaat? JoJo, you haven't lived. But I was thinking maybe a romance . . ."

"Uh-oh. We've created a monster!" JoJo said, and the girls burst into laughter.

Two hours later, the movie wrapped up and the plane was beginning its descent.

"I can't wait to see the rest of my family," JoJo confessed to Miley, bending to give

BowBow a pretzel snack through her carrier. "But honestly? I had such a blast. I wouldn't change a thing about our extended winter vacation," she admitted. "It was a surprise, but it turned out to be a good one."

"Me neither," Miley agreed. "And JoJo," she went on. "Eric gave me his email address! He wants me to choreograph a routine for him, once his ankle is fully healed."

"That's so cool!" JoJo exclaimed. "Aren't you glad you finally said 'hi'?"

"Absolutely." Miley nodded vigorously. "You know, I was brave all along. I just needed to see it for myself."

"Here, here!" shouted Michelle from across the aisle, waking her mom up. "Err, sorry, Mom!"

Well, JoJo, here we are," Mrs. Lee said an hour and a half later, when she pulled up to JoJo's driveway. "Wow! Your family goes all out with the decorations," Mrs. Lee said, sounding truly impressed as she took in the elaborate candy canes and gingerbread men adorning the house.

Just then, JoJo's mom opened the front door, and her family came tumbling out. Mrs. Lee put the car in Park and JoJo jumped out of the vehicle and ran straight into her parents' arms.

"Merry Christmas!" she shouted, as her dad lifted her up in the air and spun her around.

"Hey, kiddo," he said. "Oof! You're getting too big for this."

"We missed you tons!" JoJo's mom said. "Where's BowBow?"

"Right here," JoJo told them, reaching into the backseat for BowBow's carrier. BowBow pawed at the enclosed mesh, eager to get

out. When JoJo unzipped the carrier, her dad lifted up the little dog and pulled a miniature set of reindeer antlers from his back pocket. He placed the antlers on BowBow's head and surveyed his work. "Totally worth it," he exclaimed. "Our cute little reindeer! Now we can finally take a family photo— all five of us at the same place at the same time? Whoever would have believed it!"

"I can take it for you," offered Mrs. Lee, unbuckling her seat belt and stepping out of the car.

"That would be great!" JoJo's mom agreed. "And then why don't you come in for a minute?" She gave Mrs. Lee a significant look.

"Hey, I know that look!" JoJo said. "That means you're up to something!"

"I don't know what you're talking about," her mom protested. "Now get over here!"

She pulled JoJo close. "Let's get our Christmas wonderland in the background."

Once Mrs. Lee took the perfect shot with Miley and Michelle's guidance, everyone walked up the path toward the front door.

"Why don't you girls open the door?" JoJo's mom suggested. Now JoJo *really* knew they were up to something!

JoJo pushed the door open, with Miley and Michelle right behind her.

"Surprise!" shouted a chorus of voices. JoJo blinked. Miley's whole family and the rest of Michelle's family were all there, wrapping the girls in big hugs.

"We just couldn't wait a moment longer," Mrs. McKenna, Miley's mom, told them. "We figured we'd bring Christmas to you!"

"Since you missed Christmas Eve at home," JoJo's mom explained, "we wanted

150

to make sure you kids had the best Christmas Day *ever*."

And it was the best Christmas ever—all of it. Because JoJo had learned that friends and family were the things that united all people across all holidays. They were what made a holiday truly special, no matter where you were.

JoJo watched her friends head through the kitchen and toward the living room for another day of celebrating. Her heart was as full as it could ever be—she was so happy and filled with love, she thought she might burst. JoJo picked up BowBow and followed the others. Then she halted—right under the sprig of mistletoe that hung from the entrance to the kitchen. She looked up and laughed.

"BowBow, I don't think I tell you enough how much I love you," she told her littlest friend, holding her high in the air. Then she gave BowBow a kiss on her furry head, right under the mistletoe.

BowBow responded by licking JoJo's cheeks all over.

"Gross, BowBow! No one warned me about the slobber!"

Then she buried her head in the small dog's fur. "Merry Christmas," she told her, taking a moment to hold her close to her heart. "Now let's go party!"

More books available . . .

... BY JOJO SIWA!

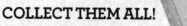